Maxine's Tree

Written by
Diane Léger-Haskell

Illustrated by
Dar Churcher

Orca Book Publishers

ON weekends Maxine and her father left the city to go camping in Carmanah Valley on the west coast of Vancouver Island. Along with other volunteers, Maxine's father built trails through Carmanah so people from all over the world could visit the ancient rainforest. Sometimes her cousin Eddie and their great-grandmother Nannie came along. Eddie helped clear the trails and Nannie came because she loved to be in the woods. Maxine was five. She was too young to work on the trail, so most of the time, under Nannie's watchful eye, Maxine played in her tree.

The sitka spruce wasn't really Maxine's tree, although she liked to pretend that it was. The tree was one of the giants of the rainforest: as wide as an elephant, as tall as the sky and as old as old could be. Ferns grew on the branches and moss crept up the trunk. The hollow at the base of the tree was so big that ten children could sit inside. Sometimes Maxine would pretend to be an animal living in a burrow or a gnome working in a tree-house. But her favourite game of all was Queen of the Forest.

One day, after playing in her tree, Maxine joined her family at the end of the trail. Her father was carefully trimming back the bushes with his long clippers. Maxine helped Eddie carry the branches off to the side of the path.

"Want to climb that hill, Max?" Eddie said.

The two children left the trail and struggled through the thick underbrush. When they reached the top of the hill, Maxine and Eddie looked out over the next valley.

The mountainside across the valley was bare. Its trees had been cut and taken away. Nothing green was left. Only ragged burnt stumps were standing.

"Uncle Syd!" shouted Eddie, "Clearcut!"

Maxine's father joined them at the crest of the hill. Together they looked at the brown mountainside.

"Dad, will that forest grow back?" Maxine asked.

"It'll be replanted," he said, "but it won't be like an old-growth rainforest. It will be only a tree farm."

Maxine frowned. "Why?"

"It takes thousands of years to grow a forest like Carmanah. All of the fungi, small plants, trees and creatures are important to the life of a forest. Here, living and dying things have always worked together undisturbed."

"Dad, will our forest be cut down?"

"It could be, Maxine," he answered "That's why we are here making trails. If people can see the beauty of a natural rainforest, they will want to save the rest of this valley."

Maxine walked slowly back to her tree. She leaned against its mossy bark as the tears filled her eyes. "Those poor trees. It can't happen to my tree. It can't," she murmured.

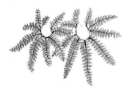

Nannie found Maxine hugging her tree. Together they sat on the old root which grew along the ground.

"What's wrong dear?" she asked.

"I don't want my tree cut down," Maxine answered sadly.

Nannie put her arms around Maxine. "This forest is a very special place," she said. "If more people come here and see how beautiful it is, I'm sure they will want to save it. We'll just have to wait and see."

Nannie kissed Maxine and went back to her knitting on the old log nearby. The little girl wrapped her arms around the big roots of her favourite tree.

"Don't worry," she whispered, "I'll save you."

Maxine thought and thought as she paced around the sitka spruce. She followed the trail to the rocky creek bed and kicked white pebbles for a while. Then, she sat on a piece of driftwood and drew shapes and letters in the sand. And then...Maxine stopped and stared at the letters.

Suddenly, Maxine jumped up and ran over to a pile of old wood. She picked up a piece of driftwood and carried it to the campsite. At the fire pit Maxine found a cold lump of charcoal from last night's fire. Carefully, she began to print on the smooth wood.

Maxine ran back up the trail to her tree and stuck the driftwood sign high up on the shoulders of the soft mossy root.

"Nannie, come see. Nobody will want to hurt someone's favourite tree," she shouted as she ran to find her father and cousin. Nannie, Dad and Eddie took a long look at her sign and smiled. Then they went back to the campsite to make their own signs.

Dad picked a western hemlock where a noisy squirrel lived. It was easy to see that it was a hemlock because its top drooped. Eddie chose the tallest tree in the country, another sitka spruce.

Nannie put her sign on a fallen cedar, called a nursing log. It was her favourite spot to sit while she knitted and kept an eye on Maxine. The old tree was covered with moss, ferns and mushrooms. Several young hemlocks grew out of it, their roots feeding on the rotting tree.

Late in the afternoon, before they left Carmanah, Maxine, her father, Nannie and Eddie stood together in the forest.

"Now there are four favourite trees." said Maxine happily.

A few weeks later, Maxine and her family returned to Carmanah. Maxine struggled to put on her knapsack. She just couldn't wait for the others to unload the jeep. She had to see if her tree was all right.

Maxine rushed down the path to the bottom of the valley and headed straight for her sitka. It was there, her sign still propped up on its root. Maxine leaned against her tree and looked around. All of a sudden, she saw a sign standing against a low branch nearby. Then another one. It was tied around a young spruce. Maxine closed her eyes, rubbed them, and looked again.

Signs were everywhere! Some were made of driftwood, others were made of bark. A few were made of beautiful cloth, with funny letters she could not read.

"Everyone has a favourite tree." she said.

Maxine ran back to her sitka spruce and gave it her very best hug. The huge root felt like a velvet cushion against her cheek. Maxine looked up. The trees of the ancient rainforest swayed gently, as their moss-covered branches reached for the sun.

Carmanah Valley lies adjacent to the Pacific Rim National Park on Vancouver Island, home to the magnificent sitka spruce and Canada's tallest known tree. The Sierra Club, the Western Canada Wilderness Committee and the Carmanah Forestry Society hope to preserve this majestic rainforest for future generations. Trailbuilding has been invaluable in creating public awareness of, and access to, the giants of the old-growth forest.

This story is dedicated to Syd, Peter McAllister and the trailbuilders.

"Save the trees for the whole wide world."
(Maxine Haskell, aged 3, September 1988.)

Copyright © 1990 by Diane Léger-Haskell (text) and Dar Churcher (illustrations)

Second printing 1992

Orca Book Publishers
PO Box 5626
Postal Station B
Victoria, B.C.
V8R 6S4

Cover design by Christine Toller

Printed in Hong Kong

Canadian Cataloguing in Publication Data

Léger-Haskell, Diane, 1957 -
  Maxine's tree

  ISBN 0-920501-38-9
  I. Churcher, Dar. II. Title.
PS8573.E35M3 1990   jC813' .54   C90-091121-2
PZ7.L43Ma 1990